Hello, Zippy!

By Jeremy Butler

Illustrated by Rashad Doucet

MASCOT BOOKS

It was a wonderful fall morning at
The University of Akron. Students were
back on campus and the football team was
about to kick off another exciting season.

Zippy was heading to the stadium for the first game of the season. Zippy noticed an important part of the mascot's uniform was missing. Where was Zippy's lucky hat?

Zippy strolled down Exchange Street, searching for that lucky hat. As Zippy walked by, Akron fans said, "Hello, Zippy!"

The mascot was feeling hungry and walked to Robertson Café to grab a good breakfast.

Zippy waited in line and asked some of
the staff if they had seen the lucky hat.
"No, Zippy, we haven't seen your hat,"
they replied.

Puzzled, Zippy sat down to enjoy breakfast. The mascot began thinking about where to search next for that missing hat.

Zippy went to the Student Union. Some students noticed Zippy approaching. They asked, "What's wrong, Zippy?"

The mascot replied, "I can't seem to find my lucky hat. Have you seen it?" The students answered, "Sorry, Zippy, we haven't seen your hat."

Zippy was now very worried. How could the mascot cheer at the football game without the hat? At Buchtel Hall, Zippy ran into two professors.

Zippy asked the professors if they had
seen the hat. They replied, "No, Zippy,
we haven't seen your hat."

Zippy continued searching all over campus for the lucky hat. It wasn't anywhere to be found!

Zippy searched and searched. The mascot asked everybody, but nobody had seen the lucky hat.

At the Alumni Center, a group of
alumni had gathered for a friendly
game of football.

Zippy asked about the hat, but the answer was the same. "No, Zippy, we haven't seen your hat," the alumni said.

At the stadium, Akron fans were getting ready for the game. They cheered, "Hello, Zippy!"

Noticing Zippy was missing the famous hat, fans asked, "Hey, Zippy, where's your hat?" Zippy could only frown.

The last place Zippy could think to look
for the hat was the Akron Zips
locker room.

And right there, sitting on a bench,
Zippy found the lucky hat! The
football team cheered, "Hooray, Zippy,
you found your hat!"

Putting on the hat, Zippy smiled from
ear to ear. As the football team was
announced, Zippy led the Akron Zips
onto the field.

Zippy watched from the sidelines and cheered for the home team. The Zips scored a touchdown!

At halftime, The University of Akron Zips Marching Band took the field. The fans stood, cheered, and sang "Akron Blue and Gold."

With great play, the Akron Zips won the football game. Zippy celebrated with the football team. Everyone cheered, "Go, Zips!"

After the game, Zippy started walking back to the residence hall. Zippy waved to Akron fans and thanked them for coming to the game.

Finally, Zippy made it back to the residence hall. The lucky hat was safely stored on a shelf before the mascot crawled into bed.

Goodnight, Zippy!

For my wife, Mehgan, and our son, Evan, as well as all
former, present and future Akron Zips. ~ Jeremy Butler

For my grandfather, Harry Fontenot. ~ Rashad Doucet

For more information about our products,
please visit us online at www.mascotbooks.com.

PRT0514B

ISBN: 1-932888-71-3

Printed in the United States.

www.mascotbooks.com

Have a book idea?

Contact us at:

Mascot Books

560 Herndon Parkway

Suite 120

Herndon, VA

info@mascotbooks.com | www.mascotbooks.com